God Doesn't

Mistakes

by Denora M. Boone

This book is dedicated to the best parents a woman could have.

Dorothy and Fred Jefferson

I love you and may the both of you rest in eternal peace.

Acknowledgements

Never can I give anyone more credit than I give God. Because of Him and His mercy I have overcome so much in life. I now understand that all of my trials and tribulations came just to prepare me for this moment in my life. God how I love you.

Special thanks goes to the man in my life Byron. Baby you have been my rock through this whole process and I thank God for giving me you. The days when I wanted to quit or thought I couldn't make this happen you were right there to push me and encourage me. I know that I can always trust you to be here through the good and bad times. You are all mine and I love you so much.

To my babies Jalen, Elijah, Mekiyah, and Isaiah you are the reason that Mommy does what she does and I thank you for being my inspiration. I made a promise to love you unconditionally and with everything that I have and I am so proud of all of you. My pudds Krystal Sheppard and Deja White. You ladies are the best friends/sisters I could ever have. God broke the mold when He created the two of you and I thank Him on a regular basis for bringing you into my life! #FFC4LIFE

To all of my sisters and brothers,

Andrea, Heaven, Shacora, NyQuan, Gerri, Miracle, Marquee, Bryce, Rory, Victor, Jessica, Jennifer, Jeremy, and James (man it's a lot of y'all!) Thank you for your love. No matter how far apart we are I know that our bond remains the same.

To my church family at Deliverance Tabernacle Christian Center in Pensacola, FL, thank you for helping me to understand the word of God, crying when I cried, laughed when I laughed, and guided me in the right direction when I felt like quitting. I love and miss y'all so much!

Special thanks to my publisher David Weaver. You took on something that most people would have been scared to do when you signed me as your first Christian Fiction author. I thank you will all that is in me for your support and encouragement. You are helping to make me greater and I absolutely love you and the rest of my new TBRS family! #SALUTE

Finally to all of the people that I could not mention I thank you for the good, the bad, and the ugly. You have helped me to remain strong and I hope I can make you proud.

Love,

Dee

PROLOGUE

Tears slowly fell from Nivea's eyes as she lay in her bed replaying the events of the night. How could something like this happen to her? She had the best of everything. The flyest designer clothes and shoes, a brand new car, big house, and best of all loving grandparents; whom she adored who cherished their only granddaughter.

"It's all my fault," she said barely above a whisper. But who could she tell what had just happened to her only three hours ago? No one would ever believe her especially after the lie she told to get herself in this mess.

Everyone would look at her funny. No one ever really sympathized with girls like her. They always thought the victim was at fault. Who wants to be looked at that way? No, Nivea would take this to her grave. If only she could wake up and this all be some horrible nightmare.

****

"All we have to do is tell your grandma that we are going to spend the night at Von's house and once we get there, we tell Candace that tonight is the big school talent show. You know she don't care what Von does as long as she has her Sour Diesel, Patron, and a man on a Saturday night!" said Dior. Nivea and Dior had been friends since head start and were more like sisters.

"Okaaayyyyy!!" Exclaimed Nivea . "But I hate that Von has to deal with seeing her mother jump from man to man like she does."

"Cha boo! You know Von don't care cause she gets to do whatever, whenever as long as her boo Quez keeps supplying Candace with what she needs."

As much as Nivea hated to admit it Dior was right. Von did as she pleased and her mother never said anything about it. Never in a million years would Mommy and Daddy, her grandparents who raised her since birth, let her get away with half of the things her friends did.

It was a surprise that they allowed her to even have a boyfriend, but considering that he was the Honorable Reverend Whittaker's grandson they allowed it.

"NIVEA!" she heard Dior yell, taking her away from her thoughts.

"Girl, why must you yell my government all loud like that? You don't know if I got warrants!"

"Cha boo! If you got warrants, I'm joining the Usher Board on Sunday," Dior laughed. "Hurry and get your butt over here so we can go. Tell Ma Fran and Pop Jimmy I said hi."

Nivea got her overnight bag and made sure everything in her room was in order and headed down the hall.

"Alright Mommy I'm getting ready to go and get Dior and head to Von's house for the weekend. Is there anything you and Daddy need me to do before I go?" she asked her grandma.

Her grandmother was the most beautiful woman she had ever laid eyes on. From her long, silky, platinum hair that touched the middle of her back, toffee colored skin that was as smooth as a baby's bottom, to her freshly manicured toes, Fran was the epitome of beauty at its finest.

"No baby you go and have fun and as always be careful. Tell my girls I said hi and give them big hugs for me. Oh and don't forget to tell Candace I can't wait to hear her sing that wonderful solo she has this Sunday for our Women's Day program."

"I will Mommy. I love you," Nivea said as she kissed and hugged her favorite woman in the world. If only she knew what 'Caramel Candace' did on her own time she would never let Nivea go over there.

As she walked to her car, she noticed her George Jefferson look-alike grandfather checking her car to make sure everything was running like it should and that it had a full tank of gas.

"You ready to roll Skoot?" he asked calling her by the nickname he had given her.

She remembered the story she was told about when she first started crawling. How he caught her scooting across the floor at 6 months old. Since that day she was his Scoot. She laughed every time he told her that story, but never got tired of hearing it.

If nothing else mattered in this world Nivea knew that her grandparents had her back no matter what. Even though she hated to tell the little white lie about spending the whole weekend at Von's, she knew she couldn't tell them what was really planned.

Her and her best girls had planned on getting all fly and meeting up with their boyfriends in Atlanta. They had planned to do everything under the sun while they were there. She had to leave now if she was going to be able to pick up her girls and take that two-hour drive from Milledgeville and be on time.

"I gotta go Daddy, but I'll see you Sunday at church."

"No you won't either. You know I don't go to that church house unless it's Christmas or Easter and I don't see no snow or boiled eggs in the grass!"

"Ohhh Daddy, you wrong for that!" she said with tears in her eyes, but she knew just how serious her Daddy was.

Just as she was about to put her car in drive, she noticed and envelope on her front seat. She opened it to find four crisp $100 bills in it and a note that read.

"Have fun Skoot, be careful, and don't tell ya mama I hit the scratch off just yet! Love Daddy."

Nivea laughed and saw the little old man who only had hair around the sides of his head and bald on top, wink his eye at her. Man she hated telling half of the truth to her parents, but as she learned in church 'A half-truth is a whole lie'. She would just repent on Sunday. It was the weekend and it was time to get it in!

Chapter One

"PREGNANT?!" screamed Gavin's father.

In all of his sixteen years living on this earth, he had never seen his father get this upset. Listening to him scream wasn't nearly as frightening as his mother's silence though. Something about the way she calmly lit her cigarette and took a sip of her favorite Brandy while never taking her gaze off of him sent an eerie chill down his spine.

His mother had been saved for as long as he could remember, but when she got beyond upset she couldn't help but smoke. It seemed to always calm her down, but this time it must have not been working because he could tell that all hell was about to break loose!

"But Pop, I swear I didn't mean for this to happen. I don't know what I'm gonna do because in less than three weeks my daughter is due."

BAM! Before Gavin could finish his sentence his mother had knocked him right to the floor and resumed her position at the Davis family's kitchen table. Jimmy knew Fran was a firecracker when she needed to be. After all, that was why he married her twenty years ago.

"Now, what I'm about to say, I intend on saying once and only once do you understand?" Fran asked her baby boy in a tone that told him how serious she was.

"Yes ma'am," was all he could muster up.

"You know how much we honor God and His Word in this house. You're only 16 years old and getting ready to be a father! Jimmy and me tried to raise you and your brother the best that we could and to teach you right from wrong.

Your brother has gone off to the Navy and you were supposed to be right behind him. How do you plan on going now with a child? We've set our eyes on that little fast tail girl Naomi only a few times."

"It's Natalie Ma'," Gavin interrupted.

At that moment, if looks could have killed, there definitely would have been some slow singing and flower bringing with him in his favorite suit!

"Now you have a baby coming in three weeks," she continued. "When that granddaughter of mine comes into this world you and Natalie better have a plan and have things in order. Do I make myself clear?" Fran finished.

"Yes mama," was all Gavin could muster up.

It was 3:30 in the morning on Christmas Eve when the phone rang. "Hello?" answered Gavin sounding like he had just swallowed a frog.

"GAVIN, COME QUICK THE BABY IS COMING!" screamed Natalie on the other end.

"THE ONLY PERSON THAT SHOULD BE CALLING MY HOUSE THIS TIME OF MORNING SHOULD BE JESUS HIMSELF!" his mother yelled from the top of the steps. She didn't believe calling someone's house later than 9pm; anything later than that was disrespectful in her book.

"Ma that was Nat," he said trying to find his clothes. "She's in labor and I have to get there."

Fran didn't want to admit that on the inside she was jumping for joy at the news of her first grandbaby being born.

"Boy its two feet of snow on that ground and if you don't want to be lying beside that girl in a bed of your own, you better put some shoes on. You'll catch pneumonia child."

Gavin looked down at his feet and realized that he only had his left sock on. He then looked back at his mother to see her beautiful smiling face.

It took them less than twenty minutes to reach Jamaica Queens Hospital and the whole way there, his mother talked to God.

"Lord I come before you right now humbling myself before you to ask that you bless my granddaughter as she comes into this world. Protect her all of the days of her life. As she grows up to be a woman Lord I ask that you never remove your hedge of protection from her.

No matter what life and this evil world tries to throw her way, I know you will not let that weapon prosper. There is purpose in her life and even if the way she got here was one I didn't agree on, I know you make no mistakes my precious Father. In your son Jesus' Holy name I pray, Amen."

Sitting in that backseat listening to that prayer touched Gavin like never before. It was normal to hear his mother pray day in and day out, but no other prayer had ever made him feel this way.

Gavin, Fran, nor his father Jimmy could imagine what they were about to encounter once they reached that hospital. Little did they know they would need God more than ever.

Chapter Two

"I'm looking for Natalie Long's room," Gavin asked the nurse at the desk. She kind of reminded him of the lady in the horror movie 'Poltergeist'. He shook that memory off because to this day that movie and her voice horrified him.

"And you are?" asked the nurse, who had a name tag that said 'Sara'.

"I'm the father of her baby. Is she here? Did she have my daughter yet? Where is she?" Gavin was rambling so his mother knew he was on the verge of breaking down. He didn't do stress or the unknown too well.

"Ma'am, is it possible to go in and see her?"

his mother said now in full control.

Sara looked at her computer screen and then back up into Fran's eyes. Before she could even speak, Fran could tell there was something seriously wrong. Sara was about to open her mouth when she saw Natalie's mother Josephine coming down the hall.

If there was one thing Fran knew, it was the fact that Natalie and her mother were just alike. Fast as hell and didn't care who knew it. And judging by the ensemble she had on she'd just finished another night at Starlight Lounge down on 125th street. Still something didn't look right in her eyes.

"Jo, is everything alright with the baby and Natalie?" Jimmy asked.

"The baby is just fine, but Nat is gone. MY BABY IS GONE! MY BABY IS GONE!" yelled Josephine. No one could really comprehend what was going on until the nurse came and pulled Fran to the side.

"Ma'am," she started.

"No, please call me Fran." Fran needed the nurse to feel as comfortable as possible.

"Well it seems as though there were serious complications during Natalie's pregnancy which caused her to lose too much blood during labor. We were able to save the baby and she is just fine, but we tried all we could for Natalie. I'm so sorry."

Fran thanked her and with that Sara walked away to the nurses' station to give the family some privacy.

Fran turned around to see Jimmy cradling Gavin in his arms as he cried. No one knew what to say or what to do. Then something hit her, where was Josephine? She looked around and she was nowhere to be found.

"Babe, where is Jo?" she asked.

"She said she couldn't take being here or seeing the baby. There would be too many memories and she just couldn't take the pain. She asked if we would take the baby once she is released and to never contact her again," Jimmy said.

Fran couldn't believe what she was hearing. *How in the world could a mother just leave like that and not have a second thought about it;* Fran thought.

Coming over again Sara asked, "Gavin, would you like to see your daughter?" Maybe once he saw his daughter it would give just a little sense of peace.

They followed the directions the nurse gave them to the nursery. When they got to the window, there was only one bassinet that sat to the right of the nurse who sat in a cherry wood finished rocking chair.

In her arms she held the most beautiful baby girl any of them had ever set their eyes on. Their eyes were so fixed on the baby they hadn't noticed one of the other nurses come to the door to let them in.

"Would you like to come in and hold her?" she asked. Gavin's legs felt like rubber and he didn't know if he could move, but with his mother on one side and his dad on the other, they were going to get through this together as a family.

Charlotte the nurse stood up to allow him access to the chair and once he sat down, she handed him his daughter. For the first time in the last hour, he smiled. Gavin smiled so hard his cheeks started to hurt, but he didn't care. She was perfect.

Her hair was thick and curly and as dark as

night. The color of her soft skin was like smooth caramel. And the smell of her instantly made him fall in love. Now Gavin understood how much his parents loved him and his brother because after one look, she was the most important thing in his life.

****

At the tender age of two, little Miss Nivea La'Rae Davis was nothing but a ball of energy. As she ran around the table in her navy blue pea coat, white dress, and her white Mary Jane shoes, she almost fell over from trying to run and laugh at the same time.

"GOTCHA SKOOT!" called out Nivea's grandfather as he brought her up in his arms. He loved his only granddaughter and couldn't imagine going a day without her. There was hesitation in the beginning about raising a newborn again, but once they got her home, it was like old times again.

"There's Mama's baby!" Fran smiled as she walked in the house. Instantly, Nivea got up and ran to her while screaming.

"MAMA MAMA!" She planted so many kisses on her mama's face they tickled. Looking into the eyes of that precious little girl made her eyes get misty.

"Come on baby don't do this to yourself. You're gonna get sick again and I can't stand to see you like that," said Jimmy.

"I can't help it, Jimmy. I still can't believe he's gone," Fran wept. It seemed like just yesterday Gavin was coming home from the corner bodega when he was hit by stray bullets.

He'd realized that his baby girl only had a few diapers left so he went to the corner to get some. There was a group of the neighborhood kids standing outside as he made his way in. There was only one brand of pampers the store had and those were the ones that made Nivea break out in a rash. *These would have to do for now*; he thought until he could go five blocks over to Pathmark.

BLATT...BLATT...BLATT!

Before Gavin could comprehend what had happened, he felt a sudden burning in his chest. Looking down, he noticed an oversized red mark on his shirt. He went to touch it, but before he could get his arm up he was being hit by another bullet and then everything went black.

By the time his parents had reached the Medical Center, it was too late. Gavin had been hit eight times in all and the fatal shot was the one to his heart. Nivea was only ten days old.

Chapter Three

"DIVAAASSSSS!" called out Von as Nivea and Dior pulled up. From the looks of it, her mother had gotten started early on her weekend because it was only four in the afternoon.

"Dang girl look at you," she said to Nivea. "Looking all 'FRESH!"

"Well you know how I do. I wouldn't do it any other way," she joked.

Even if she was the one in her group of three that carried a little more weight in all of the right places, no one could deny that Nivea was the baddest girl around. Not only was she nice to look at, she also had brains to go with it. She proudly held on to a 3.5 GPA while in her senior year at Baldwin High School.

The girls finally made their way up I-75 and in less than 30 minutes would be partying hard for the weekend. Nivea got off on the 249B exit and made her way through downtown Atlanta.

Since Von's boyfriend Quez was over twenty-one, he was able to get a suite with no problems. Dior was so excited she could barely contain herself in the backseat.

Nivea had to admit to herself that even though she knew she shouldn't be doing this, she couldn't wait to spend the entire two days with her boyfriend. Ishmael Whittaker was by far the finest 18 year-old she had ever seen. Standing just over 6 feet tall, with deep brown eyes, a head full of spinning waves, and 220 pounds of pure muscle, he was all hers!

They met each other three years ago at their

church revival where his grandfather was the Senior Pastor. Ishmael was visiting for the summer and by mid-Fall his mother had decided to move back home.

No one could imagine the massive amount of butterflies that felt more like bats in her stomach, when she looked up in the middle of her Economics class and saw him standing there. They had made eye contact and from that day on they had been an item.

In the elevator on the way up to the room "Operation She Bad" was in full effect. All outfits, make up, and hair had to be on point before they stepped off and into the room.

"OH EM GEE!" Dior squealed. This was by far the baddest hotel room ever. Come to think of it, this was her first time ever in *any* hotel room.

The room was decked out from the plush white carpet all the way down to the 6000 thread count sheets. This weekend would definitely be one of the best ones this crew had ever experienced.

"Hey there's my future wife," Nivea heard Ishmael say as he came from the back room.

"Hey you!" she said unable to contain herself from running over to him and planting a big kiss on his lips.

Ishmael and Quez helped the girls get unpacked and decided to take a couple of hours to relax before heading out later that night. This was the first time that Nivea and Ishmael would be together alone for a whole weekend.

They always went out on dates or just spent the day with each other around town and on some occasions were allowed to go to Macon to get away, but never were they allowed to spend the night together.

Nivea didn't know what to expect and she

could tell her boyfriend didn't either, but one thing for sure they were going to enjoy the time they had. Neither of them wanted to think about the consequences they would all face if word got back to their parents.

"So, what's on the agenda for tonight?" asked Nivea.

"Well tonight it's just gonna be me and you doing whatever it is that you want. Tomorrow we'll all go shopping or something and Quez said one of his boys is having a party that night," he replied.

Nivea didn't know about going to any party, but as long as she could spend time with her man she would go anywhere he wanted her to.

Dior, Quez, and Von decided to meet up with Trey who was a close friend of Quez, while Nivea and Ishmael stayed behind. About thirty minutes after the crew had gone out into the ATL nightlife, the room service Ishmael treated his queen to had arrived.

Nivea liked seeing her boo take charge and treat her like royalty. That was one of the qualities her mother loved about him. He always treated her with nothing but love and respect.

Once their meal of lobster and shrimp alfredo, steamed broccoli, salad was completed, they took showers and kicked back in their room to watch some movies. Being snuggled up with Ishmael was the best feeling ever and she wouldn't change it for the anything in the world.

"Babe?" said Ishmael.

"Yea?" she replied.

"Let's try some Moscato," he said with a sly smile. She couldn't help but giggle at the thought and sight of him smiling down at her.

"Why not? But wait, how are we going to get it? We are both under age."

"The room is in Quez's name and he's 22. They will just think it's for him anyway." Seemed like he had all the answers, so why not?

When the Moscato arrived, there was also a bowl of fresh strawberries and whipped cream to go with it. Now Nivea was no dummy, so she knew that the feeling in her stomach was a warning.

In the words of her favorite comedian Kevin Hart, "It's about to go down!"

Ishmael could tell she was nervous and to be honest, he was too. The last thing he wanted was for her to be uncomfortable around him, so he reassured her that nothing would happen if she didn't want it to. Nivea got up to open the bottle and put a strawberry in each of their glasses.

"Here," she said as she handed him is glass. "This should help the both of us relax.

Ishmael turned off the television and turned

on his IPod that was resting on its dock. He turned on a playlist that was made just for them. From Avant and Donnell Jones to Chris Brown and Ledisi; every song that meant something to them was found on that playlist.

By the time they had finished three glasses and the bubbles finished tickling her nose, Nivea was so relaxed. As she swayed back and forth to Trey Songz' melodic voice, she felt Ishmael walk up behind her. They enjoyed each other's space and before she knew it, he was carrying her to the bed.

"Oh God what am I about to do? Is this really going to happen?" she thought to herself. They both knew in their heart what was taught to them through God's word about keeping themselves until marriage, but this just felt so right.

Besides Ishmael had already let her know how deep his feelings were for her and that he wanted her to be his wife. Close enough right?

"Baby, we don't have to do this if you're not ready. I understand," he reassured her. Instead of answering him with words, she invited him to be one with her as they opened up a new world unknown to either of them.

Chapter Four

The next morning when everyone woke up, immediately they could look at Nivea and Ishmael and tell that something was different about them. It was as if they had a tattoo on their faces that read "WE HAD SEX!"

The feeling that Nivea had on the inside of her was like no other and she knew that Ishmael had the same feeling. Each time their eyes locked they couldn't help but smile.

"Unt uh, let me find out y'all got down with the get down while we were gone!" laughed Von.

"Okay!" co-signed Dior.

"Could y'all two please put the 'shut' to the 'up'? Dang y'all nosy!" said Nivea, but couldn't stop smiling if she tried.

"From the looks of it, he beat it out the park," said an unknown voice coming out of the bathroom.

Immediately at the first sight, the dude coming out in nothing but some sweats and socks, there was this eerie feeling Nivea got in the bottom of her stomach. She couldn't remember where she had seen him before, but never the less she didn't like him.

If there was one thing people knew about Nivea Davis was that she could tell what type of spirit a person had just by meeting them. Growing up in church, she knew this was called "Discerning the Spirits".

A lot of people liked to claim that this was just a way that Christians got away with judging people, but Nivea and Ishmael both knew that it was none other than the Holy Spirit letting them know something wasn't right with this character.

"From the looks of it no one asked you your opinion so just mind your business!" Nivea almost yelled.

There was something she really did not like about him, but just couldn't put her finger on it.

"Aye man, somebody better let this bit—" he started to say before Ishmael cut him off.

"Watch ya mouth my dude when you talking about my girl," he said.

"Well tell ya' girl to kill that high and mighty act and keep that attitude to a minimum," Trey said.

"The last time I checked my dad was back home in the Ville so no one tells me what to say or do. You just need to remember to keep your mouth in check when you're dealing with me!"

Nivea said before Ishmael took her into the room to get dressed and to cool off. No one could have ever imagined how those last words would cause her to test her faith level in God.

Around noon, the crew headed out to lunch and to do a little shopping. As always, Dior was on the hunt for a new man while the couples stayed locked to each other. They decided to take a break and get something to eat before finishing the mini-shopping spree.

If there was one thing Nivea loved about her friends, it was that they all got along just like family. Rarely did they ever argue, and when they did it was over just as quickly as it started.

The boys took a few minutes to head into Game Stop to check out some new videos while the girls decided to go into the Coach store. Nivea liked having nice things, but she also knew how to save her money. There was no way she would ever dream of paying $100 for just a simple change pouch. Where was the logic?

By the time they returned to the room, it was almost 8pm. Dior told them about the little cutie she met while she slipped off into the arcade whom told her about a party tonight. Considering Quez was a native of the "A" he knew pretty much everybody around his way and decided they should go.

As everyone got dressed, Nivea couldn't help getting this feeling of uncertainty that she just couldn't shake. It took her a while, but by the time they left, the feeling had subsided.

Anyone who saw the group of young teens step out of their car would consider them all to be of legal age. The boys were super clean in their all white linen pantsuits while the girls donned in similar off the shoulder linen dresses. They were the epitome of hotness tonight and knew that no one could touch them with a 10-foot pole!

Entering the club where the All White party was being held, they could see it was packed from wall to wall with people. The black light that touched every inch of the club and its partygoers gave off a certain type of ambiance that seemed to be inviting them in the instant they crossed over the threshold.

Dior walked over to the booth and gave her name to the woman sitting behind it. She scanned the VIP list and was advised to wait to the left of the entrance. Immediately Dior got nervous thinking that the woman could tell they had shown her fake ID's and was going to call the police on them.

"Girl calm down!" said Von. "You can be so extra sometimes." Before the argument about Dior being a scaredy cat could go any further, the door behind them opened and Dior's new fling appeared.

Both Nivea and Von had to admit that Dior had great taste even if she only kept her boys on her team for a hot second. She just didn't see the need to be tied down for longer than a month.

Dior's new dude was about 6'2, had deep waves, the kind that if you looked too long you would get sea sick, pretty white teeth, and the prettiest mud pie brown they had ever seen.

(Y'all know the type of mud pies that were patted down, and smoothed out just right so that you couldn't tell they were actually mud! Don't front cause y'all know!)

By the time they got in and everyone got settled, Nivea was having the time of her life. With her boyfriend by her side and close friends there, she couldn't help feeling like someone was looking at her.

It was hard to focus on anything further than five feet in front of her, but as her eyes roamed the room, the source of her discomfort became clear. It was Trey. He was staring right at her and as if he knew how uncomfortable she was, he gave her a sly devilish grin.

"Baby, I'm going to step out and get some air. I'll be right back ok?" said Nivea.

"I don't want you going out there by yourself. I'll come with you. Just let me use the bathroom and get you some water," Ishmael said with a look of deep concern on his face.

"Thanks babe," she said.

She felt like she was so lucky to have him as her boyfriend and didn't know what she would have done had she never met him.

Stepping outside into the cool night air seemed to lift the stuffy feeling she had felt while inside. She walked towards the parking lot to her car, but before she could get there, her mouth had been covered by a hand and she was lifted off of the ground. Nivea tried screaming as loud as she could, but with a hand on her mouth and blaring music on the inside it was useless.

"GOD WHAT IS GOING ON?! PLEASE GOD STOP THEM!" she yelled to God.

It was hard to tell exactly how many men were taking her away, but she knew for certain there were at least four. They threw her in a van that was parked in the very back of the lot. Before she knew it, the men had pinned down her arms and legs and taped her mouth.

She pleaded with her eyes for them to let her go, but they showed no remorse. Just then, the back door opened and Nivea thought she was being saved. Instead of someone coming to her rescue, she looked into the eyes of Satan himself.

"So, I don't hear you yappin' all that noise now, do I?" said Trey.

The absolute fear that Nivea felt could never be compared to anything she had ever felt before. Her heart pounded and the tears flowed like waterfalls down the sides of her face.

"GOD, WHERE ARE YOU?! YOU SAID YOU WOULD NEVER LEAVE ME NOR FORSAKE ME, BUT HERE I AM ALL ALONE!" she screamed in her head.

"Y'all hold this bitch still, so I can teach her a lesson!" Trey said unbuckling his pants.

"NIVEA! NIVEA WHERE ARE YOU?" she heard her friends yelling, but there was no way for her to let them know where she was.

All she could do was cry and hope they would let her go. One by one each man took their turn with her and before she knew it, they were throwing her out of the back of the van and were speeding out of the parking lot.

Chapter Five

"Here I am!" yelled Nivea coming from the opposite end of the building. After the van had pulled off, she had to think quick. How could she tell her friends, or anyone else for that matter, what had just happened to her? No one would believe her anyway.

She dusted herself off and tried as best as she could to get her hair back in order. Thank God they didn't beat her too bad or she may not have been able to hide what happened.

"Where were you? We almost called the police when Ishmael said he couldn't find you," said Von breathing hard.

Ishmael couldn't find the words to say as he

held his girl in his arms. Something just wasn't right and he could feel it deep down in his soul.

The lie that Nivea told to her friends about taking a walk around the block because she was thinking of her parents seemed to pacify her friends. They understood how she could get with the simple thought of them. Once they returned to the hotel, Nivea decided that she wanted to go home. She needed to feel safe. Home would always be her safe place.

"Ok Nivea, what's going on with you?" asked Von. Nivea just continued to stare out of the back window. She was so shook that Dior had to drive them the hour and a half back to the Ville.

"Nothing. Can you just drop it please?" she begged as the tears started falling. Before anyone could say anything else, she broke down.

"Nivea, what's wrong?' asked Von. It was

serious when her friends called her by her first name and she knew she needed to tell somebody. But what would they think of her once she told them what happened? As the tears made their way down the sides of her face, her friends moved closer trying their best to console her.

"I was raped," she said barely audible.

"What?! When?! Who?!" said Dior.

"Tonight at the club," said Nivea. She went into detail about everything that lead up to her assault and by the time she finished, Dior was crying with her while Von didn't look phased at all.

Her chest was heaving up and down so fast and her breathing so rapid that the girls had a hard time understanding everything she was trying to tell them, but they did make out the most important part. Their best friend had been raped.

***

It was seriously late when the girls pulled up
to the house, but the living room lamp was on.
What was her mother doing up this late and how
could they get past her without getting
interrogated? Dior decided to tell Ma Fran that
Nivea had gotten sick and wanted to come home.
They didn't feel comfortable letting her drive
alone, so they decided to spend the night there.

"I'm so sorry this happened to you. You
don't deserve this," said Dior as she did her best
to comfort her best friend of the last 14 years.
When Nivea hurt so did Dior and vice versa; they
were closer than any blood sisters could ever be.

"I'm sorry too," said Von. "But you do know
that you can't tell anyone right?"

"WHAT?!" said Dior almost yelling. "What
do you mean she can't tell? Those fools need to

be put away for what they did to her! I can't believe you would say something like that."

Nivea sat quietly as the two debated on the proper way of handling the situation.

"If you tell Niv that means that you will also have to tell the truth about the whole weekend. Can you imagine how much trouble we will all get into? Especially Quez, he supplied everything this weekend to a group of minors," Von stated matter-of-factly.

"Seriously Von, is that all you care about, saving your boyfriend jail time while the men who hurt our best friend runs the street?" asked Dior. Von didn't have to answer for both Nivea and Dior to know where her loyalty resided.

"Listen sis, I don't care about taking the heat for our little weekend getaway if it means helping you. I'm all in and you know that," said Dior.

Nivea had a lot of thinking to do and just needed rest. She knew it wouldn't come easy, but she tried her hardest until her eyelids finally gave in and closed.

CHAPTER SIX

"Precious Lord, take my hand

Lead me on, let me stand

I am tired, I am weak, I am worn

Through the storm, through the night

Lead me on to the light

Take my hand precious Lord, lead me

home."

Candace belted out from the bottom of her soul yet Nivea wasn't really paying attention. She didn't even want to be there this morning, but was forced to get up and come.

"It will make you feel better baby," her mother said when she came into her room.

If God was surely at church this morning where was He last night? Why didn't he stop her from getting raped and mistreated? Where was the one true God who was supposed to never leave her nor forsake her? Where was THAT God, because to her at this moment, He didn't exist.

"Lord didn't that choir sound heavenly this morning church?" asked Reverend Wittaker as he took his position behind his pulpit. For a person coming into The Very Last Harvest Church Of God In Christ for the very first time, would think that Rev. Wittaker had it all together. Little did they know, he used to be an alcoholic with a thing for many women. From the stories that Nivea had heard from a few of the church members, he was off the chain!

"Praise God" he said once the wave of "Amens" and "Hallelujahs" died down.

"Now this past week my spirit has been heavy and I couldn't understand why. So I went before the Lord in my study and the scripture Job 2:11 came to me. Can somebody read that for me?''

Sister Bernice also known as 'The Walking Bible' by the kids of the church, she was always the first one to find a scripture that Reverend called out. Some even thought she was competing to see who could find it first knowing that no one but Jesus Himself could take her on.

"Job 2:11 says, 'When Job's three friends heard about all the terrible things that had happened to him, each of them came from his home—Eliphaz of Teman, Bildad of Shuah, Zophar of Naama. They had agreed they would go together to sympathize with Job and comfort him.' OH GLORY TO GOD!" she shouted.

Nivea saw her mama roll her eyes at Sister Bernice and on the inside she laughed. There was no secret that Fran disliked Bernice and even though she didn't know the extent of it, she did know it had something to do with Daddy.

"The world we live in today is a cruel world. If you're not careful, the enemy can eat you alive," Reverend started. "He comes to steal, kill, and destroy and he will use any and every trick necessary to get you to fall. He will even use your friends."

"Amen doc!" yelled out one of the deacons.

"So, that means you have to know who you have around you. What kind of person are you calling your friend? Can you count on that person to be there when you're up and when you're down?"

Nivea may not have wanted to be there at church this morning, but something was happening to her as she sat quietly in the pew. This was one Sunday that Rev, as they all called him, had her undivided attention.

He continued, "Let me see if I can help my

youth this morning, is that alright?" There was a series of "That's alright" and "Preach Preacher!"

"In this day and time we can use the word 'friend' too much. Meaning that we call everybody our friend when in fact most of them are out to get what they can get from you and leave."

"Amen."

"So we have to be careful not to let the wrong ones in. Well, how do you know if you can really call them a friend? First you want someone around you that has morals. Although they may struggle in their walk with God, they are pressing forward nonetheless.

Next, you need someone that you can trust. A person that you know beyond a shadow of a doubt will be there when the cookie starts to crumble. If they can be there when you are at the top of your game, but not when things get hard, that's not your true friend. How many of us know someone like that?"

Almost everyone raised their hand, but the wheels were turning inside of Nivea's mind. She was thinking about who are her true friends. Could she trust them to be there for her while she was going through her situation? Only time would tell who the weasels around her were.

"Job went through a rough time in his life. Everything fell apart for him, but he stayed focused on God. I'm sure it got hard, but if you go back and read that scripture you will see that Job had three friends that came to him during his crisis."

"Yes he did," said Fran. She was paying attention to the service, but she was also paying attention to her child and her friends. Something was going on and she could feel it in her bones.

She had talked to Reverend Whittaker the

night before and asked them to come over for Sunday dinner. Maybe if she got Ishmael and Nivea in the same room she could see what kind of vibe they had.

Fran didn't stress it too much because she knew that if it didn't come out today God would reveal it when it was time. She just didn't know how explosive things were going to get once it came out. God give her the strength to endure yet another test.

"Those friends helped Job carry his burden. They helped lift him up and not once did they murmur and complain. They didn't talk about him behind his back and they encouraged him. We should have at least one friend that no matter what happens they will not leave you. A friend doesn't just tell you what you want to hear, they will be honest enough to tell you the things that you don't care to hear. That's how you can tell who has your back."

Reverend Whittaker went on about people who make you lie when you know it's wrong. The ones who make you hide things from people that could hurt them. From where Nivea was sitting if she didn't know any better she would thing he was talking about them.

As if on cue Dior leaned over and said, "Niv do you think someone found out about this weekend? I don't know about you but I sense a snake somewhere."

Nivea just shrugged her shoulders but she was thinking the same thing. One of her friends wasn't as loyal as she thought and whoever it was would be sorry once she found out.

Chapter Seven

At eleven years old Von didn't look
like your average pre-teen she looked closer to
16 or 17 years old. Her body had blossomed into
a full-grown flower right before everyone's eyes.
Her mother Candace was always complimenting
her and telling her how pretty she was and how
much of a "banger" she was, but at times Von
just wanted her mother to just tell her that she
loved her.

Secretly she envied Nivea because her mother
and father actually told and showed her how
much they loved her. And not just her but all of
her friends. Whenever they would go out to
Nivea's house for a sleepover or to hang out, the

love was felt throughout the house as soon as stepped in. Not at Von's house. But what could she do she was only 11 and still property of her mother.

She became property of her mother the day she walked into her house from a weekend getaway with Nivea, Dior, and Nivea's parents. They had had so much fun that weekend going to Six Flags and shopping and stuffing their little faces with all that they could find. Von couldn't wait to tell her mother all about it, but little did she know that weekend would be the last weekend she would be considered a child.

"VONETTA!!" her mother yelled from the dining room.

"Ma'am?" she managed to get out. Something in her mother's voice didn't sound right and instantly she was scared. Had her worst fear finally become her reality?

As she rounded the corner to the dining room, she saw her mother rolling a blunt and her mother's boss down at the "Sassy Kitty", Reginald, sitting at the table.

"He-hey Mama," she stuttered.

"Gone in there and put on the green and pink outfit I got you," Candace said without even taking her attention away from her task of skillfully rolling the blunt.

Slowly Von did as she was told. She went to the very back of the closet where she had hidden the clothes that over the years her mother had purchased for her.

The reason they were in the back was because she didn't want to take the chance of one of her friends finding them and asking her questions. That had already happened once with her little girlfriend Tangie from down the block.

"Let's play dress-up!" said Tangie all excited and before Von could object her friend was already pulling out one of her "show stoppas", as her mother called them.

"OH SNAP GIRL! My mama has one just like this, but it's in orange. She said when I turn thirteen I can use hers to get my shine on," Tangie said proudly.

Von had no idea that Tangie was being prepped to take on one of the same positions she was, but was later informed that when it became her time she better put it down like no other!

So her mother started teaching her all of the basic moves at first. The slow grind, popping her behind, just real basic stuff. As the lessons went on, the dances got more vulgar and made Von way more uncomfortable.

"Mommy, I don't like doing that one. It makes me feel nasty," she told her mother one day.

"Well newsflash little girl! If you want to eat and have a roof over your head I suggest you suck it up and get with the program before your little ass is out on the streets! And if you ever tell anybody, don't think they will believe you.

No one is gonna believe that I would ever do anything like that. Why do you think I put on such a show down at the church house? Gotta make sure my behind is straight at all times. You got it?" Candace asked while being up in her daughter's face.

"Yes, yes ma'am," she replied. She was so scared her mother would hit her she didn't know what to do. It was funny how everyone thought that her mother was this "Holier than Thou Christian" on Sunday morning, while she was droppin' it like it was hot Saturday night.

"HURRY UP VON!" she heard her mama

yell and it startled her out of her daydream.

"YES MA'AM!" she replied.

She hurried up and put on the pink bikini and neon green fishnet bodice and rushed back out into the living room. She felt so dirty doing all of the moves her mother taught her in front of this grown man who was old enough to be her father.

From that day six years ago up until now, four nights a week Von was known as "Candy Girl". It was the hardest secret she had ever had to keep and no matter how bad she needed to tell someone, she knew that she couldn't.

Her mother had told her about all of the funny looks and whispers she would get once she told and that would only be if anyone believed her. What happened at home stayed at home and only between them.

Night after night, dance after dance Von started to find herself enjoying her alter ego more. Each show was better than the last and her request started to roll in right along with the money.

On any given night she would make no less than a thousand dollars and that was after she cut her mom and Reginald their cut. No, she didn't like it at first, but she dared anyone to try and steal her shine.

She was the baddest thing walking inside of Sassy Kitty. After all, that is how she met her boo Quez. Yeah on the outside she was cool breeze, but on the inside she was a mess. A walking, living, breathing mess full of lies and no matter what she did she couldn't escape that night life. She knew this was all she would ever be because she saw her mother as her example.

No matter how many times she cried after selling her body for a few extra dollars, she knew God didn't hear her. If he did he would have protected her from all harm right? Yeah God

really dropped the ball with this one, but it was

all good.

Chapter Eight

Nivea thought about the sermon at church this morning and wondered how all of this would play out. Her mother could tell that physically her body was there, but her thoughts weren't. There was no pretending with her mother anymore either.

She knew that eventually she would get grilled, but she had to listen to Von and take her advice about not telling. She could hear the cruel comments now about how she probably wanted it or how it was her fault. No one wanted to hear that especially with the town being so small; everyone knows everyone.

Once she got into the house, she went straight to her room and closed the door. She got out of her church dress and changed back into her Hello Kitty pajamas and climbed into her California King bed. Just as she was getting to her favorite spot in the center of her bed she heard her door open and in walked Dior.

"Hey chica, how you feeling?" she asked Nivea. "I know we didn't get to really talk anymore after last night."

"I know. I guess I'm just really trying to process it all."

"Have you talked to Ma' yet?"

"Girl no! You crazy? How am I going to tell her what happened? That would mean I would have to come clean about everything. Everything D!" Nivea started to panic.

"Calm down sis, I'm right here with you unlike some people," she said referring to Von.

"As crazy as it may sound, I think I'm going to take her advice. I mean she has a valid point."

"You have GOT to be kidding me. Seriously? You need to tell the police so that he can get punished for what he did to you! I mean there might even be other girls that he has done this to and just like you they are scared."

"I mean think about it D, once we put this out there will be police involved, then the news, and once that happens everybody will know what happened. How many people do you think will believe me because we already lied about what we were doing this weekend?"

That was a good point; thought Dior to herself. She remembered one Sunday when Reverend Wittaker was talking about the man who built his house on the rock and the one who built his on the sand.

The one who built on the rock was safe when

the storm came because his house was able to withstand the rain and wind, but the man on the sand had his house destroyed. You have to start right to build right so that your end results will be right. If you start wrong, like they did when they lied about their plans, they could definitely end wrong.

"Maybe you're right," Dior finally said after thinking long and hard.

"I know I am," said Nivea

That's one thing about the devil he knows God's word too and can use it to his advantage when it's convenient for him. Neither of the girls thought about that while they were sitting there confiding in one another, but as the Father of Lies tried to work his magic, upstairs our Everlasting Father in heaven, was making his presence known to Fran.

Fran was in the kitchen finishing up her Sunday dinner of collard greens, homemade mac and cheese, cornbread, fried and baked chicken, glazed ham, rice, peach cobbler, and a chocolate cake, when she heard God's still voice.

She instantly froze when she heard Him say, "You don't have much time, but she needs you like never before."

Immediately, she understood who needed her. If there was anything Fran knew and knew well, it was the sound of the Lord's voice. Something was going on with her beautiful grandbaby and she knew it even before the girls arrived home early this morning.

It was exactly 12:21 this morning when she was awakened with the image of her baby girl with tears of terror filling her eyes. She wasted no time getting her prayer shawl and heading down to the living room so she didn't wake Jimmy.

The last thing she needed was for him to start panicking and pulling out his .38 and jumping into his old pick-up truck.

She went before God and prayed like never before. Asking Him to protect her granddaughter and let her come back home safely. She couldn't stand to lose anyone else and her health was not in the best condition.

She knew her cancer had come out of remission, but Jimmy was the only one to know. Nivea didn't need anymore stress to take her away from her studies and being a teenager. She was doing so well in school and her social life and Fran couldn't be any more proud.

With the help of God, she and Jimmy had done a fine job raising her. Fran asked God that when it was time to call her on home that he would make sure to always keep her protected and have a way of escape out of every trick the enemy meant for her.

"It is well," is what she heard God tell her and at that very moment, even though she knew there were very hard times coming to Nivea and her friends, they would all have the victory and God would get all of the glory.

****

Reverend Wittaker walked into his grandson's room to see if he was ready to go to the Davis' for dinner. With his hectic church schedule as well as other speaking engagements, he missed going to dinner with them.

Jimmy sure was a lucky man to have Fran. Even with her sickness she managed to keep him and their lovely granddaughter happy and an immaculate house. Boy if he was still in the world, he would have given his buddy Jimmy a run for his money when it came to that one.

He laughed to himself as he thought about his old days and ways, but the laughter stopped when he saw what was before him in Ishmael's room. If he had never been sicker in his life, today was the day.

Chapter Nine

For the last three weeks Nivea had really been having a hard time focusing in school. She felt like all eyes were on her and everyone knew what had happened to her. In reality, she couldn't have been more wrong because no one but the people in her tight circle knew the truth.

The more she thought back to that night the sicker she became to her stomach. Her mother had made her a doctor's appointment for that afternoon after she finished her last class.

Things hadn't been the same between her and Ismael either. There was this uncomfortable strain on their relationship and Nivea didn't know why, but before she left today she was going to get to the bottom of it.

"Ok, everyone your homework is on the board and you know that your final project is due next Thursday," said their English teacher, Mrs. Frost right as the bell rang for dismissal.

Nivea got her things and headed down the hall to find her boo. Even with all of the craziness going on with their relationship, Nivea was glad that she had a boyfriend like Ishmael. She wanted nothing more than to get back on the level they were before all of this happened. She just needed him to tell her that everything would be ok. But how could she tell him what happened to her?

"Hey baby," she said walking up to him from behind.

"Wassup?" he said with a hint of annoyance

in his voice.

"Why do you sound like that? What's wrong with you?" she said starting to feel a little irritated herself.

"I'm just surprised that you even remembered I was your man cause the only time we get is in class," he said.

"Babe, it's just been so much going on lately it's been hard to focus."

She really hoped he would let down that brick wall she could see being built. And from where she was standing it looked like she was the only one it was made for to keep out.

"Is that all you wanted?" he asked not even bothering to look her in the face.

She had been standing with him for almost five minutes now and not once had he looked at or hugged her. This was not the norm for them and it didn't feel right.

"Umm, well mommy is coming to get me for an appointment that I have today and I wanted to let you know just in case you could go with me."

She really hoped this would give them some time together and maybe, just maybe she could confide in him. The way things were coming at her left and right, she needed him to have his shoulder there in case she needed it to cry on.

"Nah boo, you good," he said and walked off down the hall.

Before he could take the left at the end of the hall, tears were cascading down her face like a waterfall. She tried to get herself together before anyone noticed and started playing 50 Cent with 21 Questions, but it was too late.

Dior and Von had witnessed the whole thing unfold and came rushing to her aid. There was something about when people come to comfort you that seem to make you cry harder. Like they had a button to push so that you could get all of the relief you needed from crying.

"Aww boo boo, it's gonna be ok," said Dior.

"I just don't know what's going on with him. With us," Nivea said crying harder. By this time, they had made it to the front office to wait on her mother to get there.

"I mean we just aren't clicking like we used to."

"What's wrong with you?" Dior asked as Nivea turned to see this perplexed look on Von's face.

"Well I didn't want to say anything to you because I thought things would blow over," Von started.

"Say what? Spill it Von," Dior said knowing this wasn't about to be good.

"Well y'all know Tangie right?"

They both thought for a minute and finally

realized whom she was talking about.

"You mean nasty Tangie? The one who they say works down at the Sassy Kitty right?" Nivea said with her nose scrunched up. Word around town was that Tangie was a stripper where Von's mother worked. She was known for sleeping around and had a bad habit of snorting cocaine and popping pills, but that was only he say/she say.

"Why y'all gotta talk about her like that when you don't even know her or her story?" Von was on the defense now.

Her friend's didn't know that she too worked at the club and both her and Tangie had been trained together. Yea what everyone said about her was true, but that didn't make it right to constantly talk bad about her. No one really knew what they faced on a daily basis and it was best that they didn't.

"Dang girl you sound like that's ya girl or something," cackled Dior.

"I don't care about all of that," Nivea said. "I want to know what you heard."

"Well Tangie said that her cousin Brandee saw Ishmael about two weeks ago. They exchanged numbers and been kickin it ever since."

"Kickin it how?" Nivea asked.

This was the part that was going to test their friendship. She knew once she spilled the whole story it was going to get ugly fast.

"Welllll," she hesitated.

"Come on Antoine Dodson, we don't have all day!" Dior was getting impatient.

"Brandee told Tangie that he came over to her house a few days after they met. They popped some pills and ended up getting down," Von lied. It was actually Tangie that Ishmael was messing around with but she had to throw Nivea off.

Nivea was frozen and didn't hear anything after that. Her stomach was doing flips and she felt that any moment the contents of her stomach would be all over the bookcase she was standing next to. It was going to be either the bookcase or her friends. Well the one she had left because Von was on thin ice right now.

"How could you keep something like this from her Von?!" Dior asked stepping closer to her.

"I didn't want to seem two-faced and Tangie begged me to keep quiet. But when I started noticing the change in Ishmael and saw what just happened now, I had to get it out." Von was close to tears by now, but she wasn't the only one who had to get something out.

Before they knew it, Nivea was getting out Wednesday's Spicy Chicken sandwich, chips, and fruit flavored water all over the place.

Right at that moment, Fran was walking through the front door and didn't waste any time turning around to head back to the car with Nivea. Von had to get home so that she could get ready for work that night.

Reginald didn't play about being late or unprepared so she had to make sure she was ready. Dior canceled her plans to spend the rest of the day with her new boy toy from Atlanta so she could be with her girl at the doctor.

Surprisingly since the night they met they had been going strong. Dior told Nivea she wanted what her and Ishmael had, but considering the current situation she wasn't too sure anymore. Only time would tell.

Chapter Ten

Once Nivea was seen at the office her doctor
wanted her to go over to the hospital to have one
last test. She needed to get an ultrasound done to
make sure her appendix wasn't the cause of her
discomfort and sickness and only the hospital
had that equipment.

They went into the outpatient center and got
settled in their room. Fran and Dior stayed by her
side every step she made. She was glad to have
them with her. The love she knew both of them
had made her feel so much better. That was until
she heard his voice.

"Good afternoon, Mr. Duncan," said the old

bald doctor. He had to be every bit of eighty years old, but for his age he looked pretty good.

"I'm Dr. Wilkins and we finally got your test results back in," he said.

The walls in the hospital seemed to be paper-thin or maybe they were just nosy. Either way it sounded like the doctor was sitting in the room with them.

"Now mind you this information only stays between us. No one will know these results unless you tell them yourself, ok?

The man on the table just nodded and waited for the doctor to go on. He wished that he would hurry up because he was supposed to be linking up with the fellas in a few. But since he got the call that he needed to come in right away for his results he made the quick stop.

"Now, all of your other test and lab work were ok, but the main one we were hoping came back negative didn't."

"Man, just spit it out, I got things I need to do," the man said.

Dior and Nivea were frozen with fear at the sound of his voice.

Fran noticed this right away, but said nothing while taking it all in.

"I'm sorry to tell you this, but you're positive for HIV."

Their ears had to be playing tricks on them. This couldn't be happening. This wasn't who they thought it was; was it?

"Man get somewhere with that mess! You trippin. I ain't got no AIDS man. I stay strapped. Trey Duncan ain't got no AIDS!!"

"Mr. Duncan I understand how this news is upsetting, but we need to start you on your treatment right away. You can very well live a long time with this disease."

Trey just stood there. He couldn't believe that this was happening. There had to be some kind of mistake. The doctor kept talking saying something about notifying the women that he had come in contact with so that they could get tested too. In the other room the girls had their biggest fear confirmed, it was Trey.

****

Fran sat quietly in the corner of the room while Dior and Nivea tried to look as calmly as they could, but she knew better. Something was wrong and now was the time to find out. Before she could open her mouth the doctor walked in.

She was a little petite honey colored woman with long flowing hair and beautiful green eyes. She looked like she belonged on the cover of a magazine instead of in those ugly green scrubs.

"Good afternoon. I'm Dr. Franklin. How are you today?" she said.

"Fine," everyone said in unison.

"Well, why don't we get started then. Is this your first ultrasound?" Dr. Franklin asked while she pulled out a computer on a table. She had all of these other gadgets hooked up to it and before they knew it, she was ready.

"First, I'm going to put this gel on your abdomen so we can get a clear picture of what's going on with you. How long have you been feeling sick?"

"Ummm, about three and a half weeks now," Nivea told her.

"And they think it might be your appendix?" she asked with this confused look on her face.

"Yea, they said that the nausea and vomiting could be caused by that."

Dr. Franklin kept her eyes focused on the

screen as she moved the probe back and forth across Nivea's stomach. The tension in the room was so thick it could be cut with a knife. Nivea looked over at her mother and saw tears beginning to form in her eyes as she looked at whatever was on the screen.

From where Dior and Nivea were seated, they didn't have access to view it, but whatever it was that made her mother cry had to be bad.

"Looks like we found the source of the problem," the doctor said.

A look of relief came across Nivea's face. No one could prepare any of them for what was about to be revealed. Dr. Franklin turned the screen towards Nivea and Dior broke down crying. Confused Nivea looked around the room.

"What's going on?" she asked getting scared.

"Nivea looks like you're about five weeks

pregnant."

Both Nivea and Fran's hearts dropped to their stomachs at the exact same time.

To be continued..............

Nivea and her friends seem to be facing challenge after challenge and blaming God for each and every one. Who is the father of Nivea's baby and could it be possible that God hates her enough to allow her to catch HIV from the man that raped her?

What is the secret that Ishmael and Dior both hide and will Von's double life come to the surface? Trials come to make us stronger no matter how bad they hurt us but it's all ordained by God for our good. No one likes to go through the bad times, but after all, a diamond can only exist if there is enough pressure.

Made in the USA
Middletown, DE
19 September 2015